ZAC POWER

| 24 HOURS TO SAVE THE WORLD ... AND CLEAN HIS ROOM |

SHOCKWAVE

BY H. I. LARRY

ILLUSTRATIONS BY DAN McDONALD

hardie grant EGMONT

CHAPTER... ...ONE

Zac Power was not happy. First of all, it was raining. If that wasn't bad enough, it was also really cold. But to top it all off, Zac's class was doing a cross-country run.

Why can't I be somewhere warm and dry, instead of here? thought Zac, picking up his running vest. The vest felt really heavy as he pulled it on over his head. *Great*, he sighed to himself. *My vest feels like it's made of lead, and I have three kilometres to run!*

BANG! The starter pistol sounded and the runners took off.

Zac struggled not to streak in front of his classmates. He was a really fast runner, but he knew he had to fight the urge to speed ahead. His dad always gave him the same warning before a race. 'Look ordinary, Zac! You mustn't let people see what you can *really* do.'

Because not only was Zac an excellent athlete, he was also a top spy. In fact, everyone in his family was a spy, even his geeky brother Leon. But all their spy training, special missions and high-tech gadgets were top secret. Not even Zac's closest friends had any idea that he was the number one spy for the Government Investigation Bureau, or GIB for short.

Soon Zac's sneakers were wet, and he was covered in mud up to his knees.

The sooner this race is over, the better! Zac muttered to himself. The rain seemed to be getting heavier by the second.

Then Zac had a *really* weird feeling. It felt like an invisible force was pulling him off-course and into the bushes. *I must be losing my balance*, thought Zac, making a mental note to do some extra balancing poses in his next karate class.

He ran back onto the path and kept jogging. But there it was again! He felt like he was being pulled towards a magnet. Zac's spy senses tingled. *Something's up!*

He looked down at his rain-speckled vest. *It's just like everyone else's, isn't it?*

Then Zac took a closer look. *Hang on... they're not raindrops,* he realised. *They're LEDs! I must be wearing an ImpelloVest.*

Zac had heard about this latest GIB

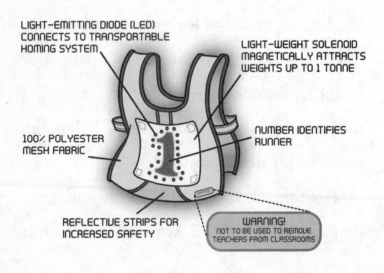

LIGHT–EMITTING DIODE (LED) CONNECTS TO TRANSPORTABLE HOMING SYSTEM

LIGHT–WEIGHT SOLENOID MAGNETICALLY ATTRACTS WEIGHTS UP TO 1 TONNE

100% POLYESTER MESH FABRIC

NUMBER IDENTIFIES RUNNER

REFLECTIVE STRIPS FOR INCREASED SAFETY

WARNING!
NOT TO BE USED TO REMOVE TEACHERS FROM CLASSROOMS

gadget from Leon, who worked with the GIB inventions squad. ImpelloVests were designed to pull the wearer in a particular direction.

Zac stopped fighting the pull of the vest. He didn't know where he was going, but he figured he'd find out sooner or later.

Sure enough, the vest steered Zac towards a car that was partly hidden by some bushes. Zac recognised the small GIB logo on the number-plate.

GIB must have a mission for me, thought Zac. Often going on missions was annoying. But today he didn't mind. *I'm going to miss half the cross-country run! Even better, mum won't be able to hassle me about tidying my room this afternoon.*

But as Zac got closer to the car, his grin faded. As GIB's top spy, he was used to the best gadgets, the fastest subs, the latest technology. So *why* was there a clapped-out old car waiting for him?

The car was huge, rusty and really dirty.

Zac took a deep breath, and tried not to be too disappointed as he opened the car door.

A good spy is never caught off guard, but Zac was totally surprised by what he saw. It may have been rusty on the outside, but inside the car was another story.

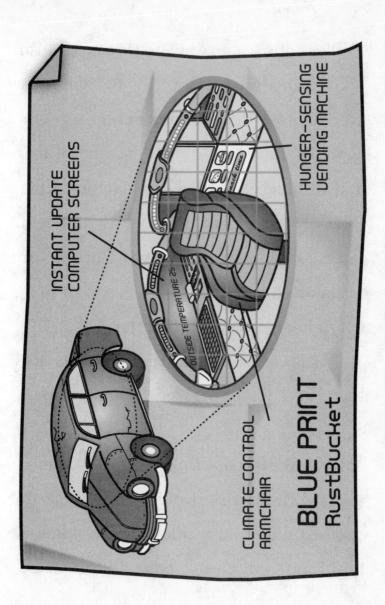

BLUE PRINT
RustBucket

INSTANT UPDATE
COMPUTER SCREENS

HUNGER-SENSING
VENDING MACHINE

CLIMATE CONTROL
ARMCHAIR

The entire cabin was lined in super-plush carpets and leather. Covering the windows were latest-design computer screens showing location, outside temperature, and distance to GIB headquarters. One window was constantly showing new release movies. Built in to one of the car walls was a vending machine, with a long list of food and drinks on offer.

RustBucket outside, dream-machine inside, thought Zac, impressed. *What a perfect disguise!*

'Good afternoon, Agent Rock Star,' said a computerised voice. A robotic arm reached out from a side panel, holding a towel and some clean clothes. 'Please make yourself comfortable. We have a long drive ahead of us.'

Zac dried himself off, and quickly changed into the cargos, hoodie and cool new sneakers.

Then he sank into the RustBucket's deep, comfortable leather armchair. There was no question that GIB knew how to do things. There was also no question that Zac was about to be sent on yet another dangerous mission.

So really the only question was, hot chocolate with marshmallows or milkshake with sprinkles?

CHAPTER... ...TWO

'Are you ready for your StratoLance training, sir?' inquired the computerised voice, as the car drove off.

'Totally ready!' replied Zac.

The StratoLance was the GIB's latest, fastest scramjet. Leon couldn't stop raving about it.

'You'll find the flight simulation disk in the pocket of your cargo pants.'

If I pass the simulator training, maybe they'll let me fly the real thing! thought Zac.

He grabbed a packet of M&Ms from the vending machine and then slipped the game disk into his SpyPad. The SpyPad was the personal computer, gameboy, electronic communicator and personal assistant issued to all GIB spies.

WHIRRR! KER-LICK!

A safety harness and flight joystick suddenly snaked out from the back and arms of Zac's swivel armchair. He strapped in and put on a set of headphones.

The computer screens lining the cabin now displayed a picture of the runway of GIB's top-secret airfield. Overhead panels slid back to reveal aircraft gauges and dials. The car's interior now looked like the cockpit of a StratoLance!

This is the most realistic flight simulator I've ever used! Zac thought, as he fired up the jet engines. He pushed the joystick forward. Instantly, the virtual StratoLance felt like it was taking off.

As he whooshed upwards, strong G-forces plastered Zac into his seat. He didn't fight them. Gradually the G-forces pulled back, and the computer display sky turned from blue to deep purple. Everything that was not bolted down began floating around the car.

This simulator also has Sim Micro-Gravity! realised Zac. *Let's see what else it can do.*

Zac slammed the joystick forward. Instantly, the plane screamed into an extreme dive. The gauges spun madly and the display panel showed the simulated ground rushing up towards him.

Zac waited until the nose of the virtual *StratoLance* was almost touching the ground.

Only then did he yank the joystick back and zoom upwards.

Not bad at all! chuckled Zac. Then he put the plane through its paces. He looped and twirled through the air, testing out all its functions and features.

Finally a message flashed up on his screen. 'Time's up. Return to the airfield immediately!'

Zac checked his watch. Four hours had already passed!

That sure is a good way to pass a long car trip! thought Zac.

As he made his descent, the car's gravity levels returned to normal and all the free-floating stuff hit the floor with a thump. A single black M&M plopped right into Zac's hand as he made a perfect landing.

The car's door slid open, and Zac found himself at GIB's top-secret airfield. It was still raining hard.

'Agent Rock Star, congratulations on getting the highest marks ever for the StratoLance flight training,' said Agent Tripwire, who was waiting for him on the tarmac. 'Now, please activate your mission disk.'

■■■■■■■■

CLASSIFIED
FOR THE EYES OF ZAC POWER ONLY

MISSION INITIATED 3:00PM

The World Council of Nations has just received this threat: Pay $500 billion in ransom or a purple diamond LaserBlaster will be used to set off shockwaves around the world. You have until 3pm tomorrow.

YOUR MISSION

- Go to the Wild Savannah.
- Find out exactly what is going on at the purple diamond mine.
- Locate and deactivate the LaserBlaster by 3pm tomorrow.

Mine co-ordinates: 04.25° South 34.33° East

MISSION TIME REMAINING:
19 HOURS AND 45 MINUTES
END

SIM MICRO-GRAVITY
>>> OFF

Zac glanced down at the M&M in his hand. Of course! It was the mission disk.

'Purple Diamonds are valued for their beauty, but they can also be used in cutting-edge laser technology,' explained Agent Tripwire. 'They're only found in one diamond mine, deep in the Wild Savannah. Yesterday the mine's owners reported that the diamonds from the mine have disappeared!'

'Well, the Wild Savannah is on the other side of the world!' exclaimed Zac. 'I'll need to get started straight away.'

'Exactly,' agreed Agent Tripwire, as a hover-pad skimmed over to pick them up. 'You'll have to use speed and cunning for this mission. The Wild Savannah is one of the most dangerous places on earth.'

It might be dangerous, thought Zac, as they sped off through the drizzle towards a distant hangar, *but at least it'll be sunny!*

CHAPTER... ...THREE

The hover-pad zipped into the huge hangar. It stopped under the sharp nose of the most awesome aircraft Zac had ever seen.

Wow! The real StratoLance! Zac thought. He recognised it instantly from Leon's favourite nerdy magazine, *Spy Stuff Weekly*. The cockpit hatch was open, ready for some lucky pilot to take the controls.

Will it be me? wondered Zac.

He imagined climbing in, doing the pre-flight check, firing up the engines…

'Concentrate, Agent Rock Star!' said Agent Tripwire sternly. 'I'm relaying key mission data. Firstly, the Wild Savannah is on the far side of the world, so you'll fly the StratoLance solo to save travel time.'

'Yes!' said Zac, punching the air.

'Secondly, you've already lost some vital hours while completing the flight training,' continued Agent Tripwire, 'so you will have to fly at top speed.'

'No problem,' grinned Zac.

'And thirdly,' added Agent Tripwire, 'although the purple diamond mine is under GIB's Big Eye satellite surveillance 24/7, no suspicious activity has been detected. Yet the diamonds keep disappearing. Strange, huh? We suspect an evil genius at work here. Extreme caution is required!'

'Of course,' Zac shrugged, a bit annoyed. Sometimes it felt like the other GIB spies forgot that he wasn't just some kid. After all, he was top of the GIB Spy Ladder, week after week!

Then Zac noticed a strange machine nearby. It looked like a cross between a space suit and a robot. People in white lab coats were working on it.

'An inventions squad member will brief you on some special tools to help you with this assignment,' said Agent Tripwire. 'You know Agent Tech Head, of course.'

'Hi, Leon,' said Zac, as his brother walked over. 'What does that do?' Zac asked, pointing to the mysterious robot-suit.

'That,' Leon said, sounding proud, 'is my latest masterpiece, the ExoSkeleton suit! This mission will be dangerous and technically difficult. You're going to need the best protection we can give you.'

Agent Tripwire nodded. 'When you reach the Wild Savannah you'll have to eject from the StratoLance from low space and parachute to earth,' he said. 'The Savannah itself is teaming with ferocious animals. Then there are all the active volcanoes.'

'And let's not forget the LaserBlaster's shockwaves,' added Leon. 'GIB still don't know exactly what these do, but we suspect they have the ability to disable communication systems worldwide!'

Zac looked closely at the ExoSkeleton. The heavily armoured suit had massive arms and legs. Power packs bulged all over the body. The helmet had a head-up display screen. All the controls were built in to the bodywork.

'It looks cool enough,' Zac said. 'But what does it do?'

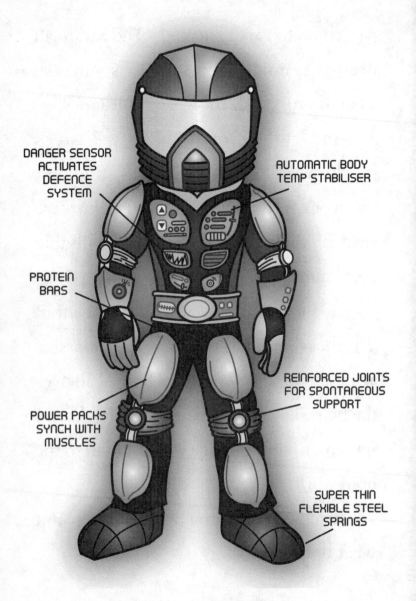

DANGER SENSOR ACTIVATES DEFENCE SYSTEM

AUTOMATIC BODY TEMP STABILISER

PROTEIN BARS

REINFORCED JOINTS FOR SPONTANEOUS SUPPORT

POWER PACKS SYNCH WITH MUSCLES

SUPER THIN FLEXIBLE STEEL SPRINGS

'What *can't* it do!' Leon exclaimed. 'The suit senses electrical signals in your muscles and multiplies your strength. It detects danger and forms a protective barrier – even before you know you need it! You'll run faster than an Olympic athlete, and jump four times your own height. Plus it's bullet-proof and crash-proof!'

With help from his brother, Zac clicked the suit on over his normal clothes. Although it looked bulky from the outside, once it was on it felt as comfy as pyjamas.

ZAAAP!

A tingle raced up his spine as the ExoSkeleton synched with his muscles.

Zac's arms and legs tingled with power. He couldn't resist leaping into the air and doing a somersault. He barely bent his legs as he jumped, but he sprang right up to the ceiling of the hangar anyway!

'Hey, be careful!' squeaked Leon. 'If you must do gymnastics, use this SpiderPak.' Leon handed Zac another gadget. 'Looks like an ordinary belt, doesn't it? But press the green button and it shoots out a nano-tube silk line. The line is 200 times stronger than steel, but is practically invisible.'

'Time to go!' interrupted Agent Tripwire. 'It's already 8pm. You've got less than 19 hours to complete this mission.'

Zac slipped on the SpiderPak belt and

pressed the green button at the side of the buckle.

ZZZZZZZZZZZ**ZZZZZZ**T!

A long silver jet shot out and stuck to the StratoLance's cockpit. Thanks to his new powerful arms, a tug on the line was all Zac needed to scramble up into the pilot's seat.

This mission's going to be a total blast! decided Zac, firing up the jet engines.

CHAPTER... ...FOUR

Zac steered the StratoLance onto the runway. The flight program disk was already loaded into the on-board computer, so Zac ran through the pre-flight control checks.

'Control to Agent Rock Star, you are cleared for take-off!' announced the tower.

Everything outside the cockpit went blurry as the StratoLance gathered speed. In seconds, the plane headed for the sky.

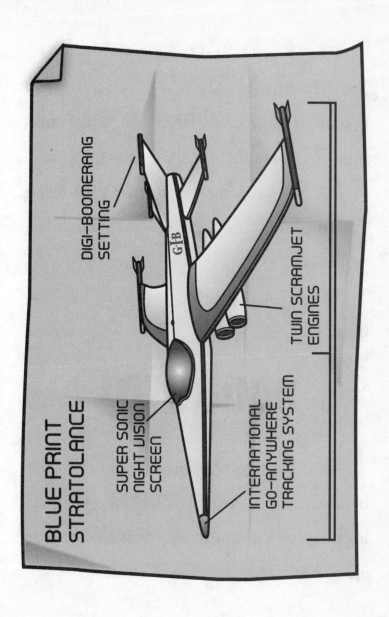

BLUE PRINT
STRATOLANCE

DIGI-BOOMERANG
SETTING

SUPER SONIC
NIGHT VISION
SCREEN

TWIN SCRAMJET
ENGINES

INTERNATIONAL
GO-ANYWHERE
TRACKING SYSTEM

Next stop, the Wild Savannah! grinned Zac. The StratoLance was heavy to fly, but thanks to the ExoSkeleton suit, Zac's new muscles made the controls easy to tame.

Just how fast can this thing go? wondered Zac, pushing the joystick as far forward as he could.

The jet accelerated faster and faster, until…

BOOOOM!

What was that? Zac quickly checked the head-up flight display. *Hey!* he grinned, looking at the controls. *That was a sonic boom. I've broken the sound barrier!*

Soon Zac was travelling through the upper atmosphere. When the altimeter showed he was cruising on a low space course, Zac finally levelled the jet out.

Now I can just kick back and enjoy the ride for a while, thought Zac, looking at the view.

Up this high, it didn't feel like the StratoLance was moving at all. But the airspeed read-out showed the current speed to be Mach 6 – six times the speed of sound!

Below the jet, Zac could see the earth's curve with the lights of hundreds of cities twinkling like jewels. *I wonder how many kids down there would like to swap places with me right now!* chuckled Zac.

While the StratoLance was cruising in low gravity, Zac tried out the dives, rolls and loops he'd practised in the simulator. The acrobatics were even easier now he was wearing the ExoSkeleton suit! Zac could do amazing stunts with a flick of his wrist.

Zac put the StratoLance into autopilot and dozed for a few hours.

Suddenly, Zac's headphones buzzed. 'Control to Agent Rock Star!' said Ground Control. 'Time to target is  30 minutes! Drop back your airspeed!'

'Affirmative!' Zac replied.

Time flies when you're flying! thought Zac, checking his watch.

Then he touched the computer display to bring up the instructions on ejecting from the jet.

On command, press the eject button on your left. As you eject, your ExoSkeleton suit will go into Full Protection Mode to ensure your safety.

'Entering the drop zone!' warned Ground Control. 'Eject! EJECT!'

Zac slammed his hand down on the flashing eject button. Instantly, he dropped through the floor of the StratoLance.

As he hit the air, the ExoSkeleton pulled Zac into the brace position. He felt the armoured plates interlock around him.

'Freefall speed is 2000 kilometres per hour!' reported the ExoSkeleton's built-in speedometer.

Zac had jumped out of planes hundreds of times before, but never from 60 kilometres up.

So this is what it's like to be a meteorite! he thought, as the land, clouds and sea rushed up towards him.

Safe inside the insulated shell of the

ExoSkeleton, Zac saw the suit's outer skin glowing fiery red as it hit the thin, high-altitude air.

Suddenly, tiny jets fired up from behind his ankles, instantly slowing the descent.

WHUMP!

A massive parachute billowed out and Zac began drifting gently to earth. As he floated, the suit unlocked and uncurled. Zac checked out the view.

Below him, dawn was just breaking over the Wild Savannah. Giant volcanoes glowed on the horizon like angry, red pimples. Tiny specks of colour moved across the land. From up here, they looked like ants. But Zac knew they weren't. *Wild animals!* he thought, with a shiver of excitement.

As he drifted closer, Zac could see the animals more clearly. To his left was a herd of giraffes. To his right was a vast waterhole, filled with hippos. And directly below him was a group of grazing rhinos!

Leon said this ExoSkeleton is bullet-proof and crash-proof, remembered Zac. *But is it rhino-proof, too? I guess I'm about to find out!*

CHAPTER... ...FIVE

THUD!

As Zac hit the ground, his parachute instantly folded into the ExoSkeleton. The herd of rhinos looked up at him, surprised. At the front was a very cranky bull rhino. He lowered his evil-looking horn and pawed the ground.

Zac leapt to his feet and took off. The ExoSkeleton meant he could run at double his normal speed. But all the same, the huge creature was gaining on him.

As he ran, Zac fumbled for his SpyPad. Then he called his brother.

'Uh, Leon? Quick question,' he yelled into the phone as he tore along. 'Can the ExoSkeleton out-run an angry rhino?'

'No,' replied Leon calmly. 'Don't run! Stand completely still.'

Zac could hear the angry snorts of the rhino right behind him. *Stand still?* Was Leon insane? It went against every instinct in Zac's body.

RHINOCEROS

DANGER!
CAN WEIGH UP
TO 2 TONNES
VERY IRRITABLE!
EXTREMELY AGILE

DANGER

But Leon has watched all 200 episodes of Creepy Creatures, reasoned Zac. *Some of them twice! Maybe I should do what he says…*

Zac skidded to a stop and stood completely still.

The huge rhino stopped, too. Then it stomped around, looking puzzled.

To Zac's astonishment, the rhino wandered right past where Zac was standing, and sniffed the air. It came so close that if Zac had reached out his hand, he could've easily patted it. But Zac didn't plan on doing that!

Instead, he held his breath and waited. Surely any minute now the rhino would gore him with that nasty-looking horn!

But after a few moments, the rhino turned around and wandered back to its herd.

Zac waited until the herd walked off. His heart was still pounding. Then he called Leon again.

'What just happened?' Zac asked. 'Does this suit make you invisible or something?'

'No,' replied Leon. 'Rhinos have a great sense of smell, and incredible hearing. But their eyesight is terrible. The ExoSkeleton is made from a special, non-odour-absorbing plastic polymer, so I knew he wouldn't be able to smell you. But he could hear you running! I figured if you stopped moving, the rhino would think you'd vanished.'

'Nice one, Leon!' chuckled Zac. He had to hand it to his brother. He sure knew a lot of useful facts. 'Anything else I should know about the animals around here?'

'I installed an *Animals of the Savannah* patch to your SpyPad last time I serviced it,' said Leon. 'Whenever you see an animal you want to know more about, just hold up the SpyPad and let it do a scan. You can also switch on a Native Animal Warning Mode. If a herd of elephants is near, the SpyPad will beep three times. Two beeps means rhinos. Lions are one big, long beep.'

'Thanks, Leon!' said Zac.

'Oh, yeah,' added Leon. 'One more thing. Mum says that just because you're on an incredibly dangerous mission doesn't mean you're excused from cleaning your room. It has to be done by dinner time.'

Zac sighed. 'Tell her I'll get it done.'

Zac switched on the Animal Warning Mode as he hung up. He checked the time.

He only had eight hours to complete the mission. But where should he go? The Wild Savannah was a huge place. The LaserBlaster could be anywhere!

I'll head for the purple diamond mine first, decided Zac. *If the diamonds are being stolen from there, I may find some clues that lead to the LaserBlaster.*

Zac checked his current location. *I'm 100 kilometres off-course!* he realised. *Looks like a cross-country run today after all.*

Zac gulped down some high-energy protein bars stored in the ExoSkeleton's hip compartment. They tasted a bit like rubber, but Zac knew he couldn't be fussy.

It'll be a two-hour run to the mine, calculated Zac, switching the ExoSkeleton into Marathon Mode. *I need all the energy I can get!*

CHAPTER... ...SIX

Zac ran along easily at a pace that would

have qualified him for the Olympic 500

metres sprint.

Cool. He was making great progress.

Suddenly, the SpyPad beeped three times. *There must be elephants nearby,* thought Zac, remembering the wild animal code. But where? Then he heard the urgent cries of an animal in distress.

Better check it out! he decided.

Zac slowed down and pushed through a thorny hedge. Up ahead he saw a swamp. Right in the middle was a baby elephant, sinking fast.

Quicksand! thought Zac, with a shudder of fear. It wasn't the first time he'd tried to get something out of quicksand, but he *really* hoped it was the last!

A mother elephant was standing to one

side, desperately trying to pull her baby out of the sticky mud with her trunk. But the harder she pulled, the more the calf sank. It was terrible to watch!

Zac knew time was ticking away on his mission, but he couldn't just leave a baby elephant to sink into the quicksand!

Zac took a deep breath and waded into the thick, oozy, stinky mud.

Here's hoping Leon's nanotube silk is as strong as he says it is! Zac thought, as he activated the SpiderPak belt.

SWOOSH!

A thin silver jet shot out from the belt and wrapped around the poor calf. Zac fired off more nanotubes, until a thick web surrounded the baby. Then, with his powerful ExoSkeleton arms, Zac tugged on the web and slowly backed out of the mud. It was like walking in half-set concrete!

SSSShlur-Splat!

One very wet and frightened baby elephant popped out of the mud.

Zac clicked the SpiderPak to release the nanotubes. Straight away, the baby trotted back to its fretting mother. Then they hurried off to join their herd.

Better get to the mine ASAP! thought Zac, standing up. He was covered in stinky mud, but he knew he had to keep running towards the mine. He checked the setting on his ExoSkeleton suit to make sure it was still on Marathon Mode.

Uh oh! The suit had other ideas. It made a spluttering sound and then blew sparks into the air. The quicksand had short-circuited the suit's electronics!

WARNING!
NOT MUD-PROOF

Zac wriggled out of the suit, and put the SpiderPak belt around his waist.

Looks like I'll have to run the old-fashioned way! he sighed. *Lucky it's not too much further.*

Finally, Zac found himself at the high razor wire fence that protected the mine. Across the locked gateway was a big sign.

PURPLE DIAMOND MINE

Zac let himself in using his GIB-issue skeleton keys. But he stopped just inside the gates. His spy senses were tingling.

I better find out all I can about this place before I go any further, decided Zac.

He called Leon.

Naturally, Leon knew everything there was to know!

'The mine is run entirely by remote control,' said Leon. 'The owners operate it via satellite monitoring. But something strange is going on. It's been weeks since the automated mining machines have found any diamonds.'

'Maybe the supply has dried up?' suggested Zac.

'No,' replied Leon. 'Their diamond radar equipment says there are still plenty of diamonds in the ground. But somehow, they vanish before they reach the surface.'

Zac frowned. Whoever was pulling this off was obviously pretty nasty. And very smart! *It sounds like the work of Dr Drastic,* thought Zac suddenly. It had been ages since he had thought of Dr Drastic.

But I cured Dr Drastic's evilness on my Poison Island mission, thought Zac, shaking his head. *He couldn't be behind all this.*

Zac looked around for clues. To his right were some old buildings. To his left was a flock of birds, standing around the mine's entrance.

As Zac watched, the entrance opened and mining machines trundled out, dumping rocks and earth onto a nearby heap.

Zac checked out the machines with interest. *They must be the automated mining machines,* he thought. Along the side of them was written *Mine Master*.

They all had heavy-duty drills at the front, as well as a scoop. At the back they had a tray with a sieve across it.

They must dump the earth they've dug up onto that sieve, realised Zac. *The earth falls through, leaving the diamonds on top.*

Once the Mine Masters had finished unloading their rubble, they drove back into the mines.

It was weird watching them move along without any drivers. But everything at the mine seemed OK.

Just to make sure, Zac put his SpyPad into Danger Mode and scanned it around. To his surprise, when the SpyPad passed over the birds near the mine entrance, it began beeping furiously!

It's probably an error, Zac frowned. But just to be sure, he scanned one of the birds again.

Warning!
Not a carbon-based life form.

Zac looked at the read-out in surprise. *What's going on? All living things are carbon-based, aren't they?*

I'd better take a closer look, decided Zac.

But he'd only taken one step forward when suddenly the air was full of flapping wings and ear-piercing screeches.

Bird strike!

CHAPTER... ...SEVEN

Zac ducked and scrambled for cover. Once he was a few metres away, the birds settled down again.

There's something totally weird about those birds, thought Zac. *I've got to catch one and check it out.*

Zac rummaged around in the pockets of his cargo pants. GIB had packed them full of things that might be useful in the

Wild Savannah – insect repellent, head-torch, a floppy hat with mosquito netting across it.

'Perfect!' thought Zac, when he saw the net. Then he stepped towards the flock.

The things I do for GIB! he muttered to himself, as the birds flew up around him again. *Turning myself into bird-bait!*

Swoosh! A bird dived straight at his face. Zac flipped out the net and neatly caught the bird. 'They might be vicious,' he chuckled, moving back a few paces, 'but they're not very smart.'

Zac removed the struggling bird from the net and turned it over. On its belly was an on/off switch.

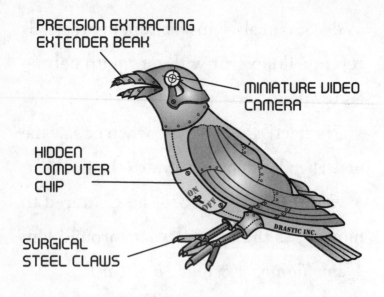

PRECISION EXTRACTING
EXTENDER BEAK

MINIATURE VIDEO
CAMERA

HIDDEN
COMPUTER
CHIP

SURGICAL
STEEL CLAWS

Zac flicked the switch off, and the bird stopped struggling. Now Zac could examine it easily. Under its tail were the words *Drastic Inc*.

Zac stared at the bird. If Drastic really *was* involved in this plot, there was no time to lose. *I've got to get into the mine right away and see where those diamonds are going!* he thought.

But how was he supposed to get into the mine? There was no way those robo-birds would let him past.

Maybe there's another way into the mine, thought Zac. He switched the SpyPad into Soil Scan Mode and scanned the ground around him.

When he pointed it at a nearby rock, the SpyPad's screen flashed.

Zac ran over and carefully pushed the rock aside. Sure enough, below it was a deep hole. It was very narrow and the edges were crumbling.

This will have to do, thought Zac, grimly, lowering himself into the hole.

WOOOOSH!

Zac felt his stomach lurch as he slid down the mine-shaft. It was like being on the longest, rockiest slippery-dip ever!

It was a very tight fit, too. Zac's arms were pinned to his sides as he shot down, feet first.

If this shaft gets any narrower, I'm going to be stuck like a cork in a bottle! thought Zac nervously.

Luckily, a moment later, the shaft spat him out with a thud into a large cavern.

It was really hot down there, and it wasn't long before Zac was dripping with sweat. *But there's no time to complain*, he realised, checking his watch.

He had to keep moving – he had just two hours till the LaserBlaster went off!

Zac fumbled in his pockets and pulled out his head-torch. Just then, he heard a noise.

Moments later, a Mine Master trundled down the tunnel and started drilling at the walls.

At first, it didn't seem to dig up anything other than rocks and dirt. Then Zac saw something sparkling in the wall.

A purple diamond! Zac gasped. The diamond looked amazing surrounded by rock — much better than on someone's finger!

Zac swung his torch around to look at the back of the Mine Master. There was a flock of robo-birds sitting on its tray. They looked really creepy, with their eyes lit up like bright yellow headlights in the dark.

No wonder those birds were hanging around

the mine entrance, thought Zac. *They must be hitching rides down here on the Mine Masters!*

The robo-birds seemed to have sensed the purple diamond. In a flash, a bird swooped over and hovered in front of the earth wall. It began digging around the gem, using its beak as a high-powered drill.

Seconds later, it pulled the diamond out of the wall and swallowed it! Instantly, the robo-bird's eyes changed from yellow to purple.

So that's *what's going on!* thought Zac triumphantly. *Dr Drastic must be using these robo-birds to steal the gems from the Mine Masters.*

Now all I have to do is follow this bird to see where it goes next. I bet it will take me straight to Dr Drastic...and probably to the LaserBlaster as well!

But before Zac could go anywhere, the ground began rumbling. Huge rocks started falling down around him.

Uh oh, thought Zac. *Cave-in!*

CHAPTER... ...EIGHT

Zac crouched down while the rocks fell around him. The noise was deafening, and his lungs filled with dust.

Finally, the cave-in stopped. Once the air cleared, Zac shone his head-torch around. He was trapped!

I've got to get out of here! thought Zac. *But how?*

For the first time, Zac started to worry

about this mission. Dr Drastic's deadline was looming, and Zac was stuck in a cave with a Mine Master and a robo-bird full of diamonds!

Zac took a thickness reading of the rock fall with his SpyPad.

On one side the blockage was 15 metres thick, and on the other it was ten. It would take hours to mine through that.

Then Zac scanned the floor.

Hey! The floor's only five metres thick, he realised. *There's probably another tunnel below this one.*

Zac's mind started ticking over.

He ran over to the Mine Master and flipped the controls to 'manual'. Then he pulled the drill towards the ground.

BAM-BAM-BAM!

The Mine Master pounded the floor, and rocks went flying. Finally, the Mine Master's drill broke through the ground.

'Whoah!' gasped Zac, as a blast of steam hissed up through the hole.

He had tapped into a boiling underground river, super-heated by red-hot volcanic rocks!

Most spies probably would've given up at this point. *But you don't stay at the top of the Spy Ladder every week by giving up!* he reminded himself.

One of his granny's cheesy sayings popped into his head.

WHEN IN TROUBLE, JUST GO WITH THE FLOW
— Zac's Granny (Agent Wrinkles) —

G·I·B

Zac ran his eye over the Mine Master. Was there anything on it that could help him out?

Yes! The side panels! They were made of heat-resistant, super-strong Kevlar. And they were even sort of shaped like a surfboard.

Perfect! grinned Zac, unbolting a panel with the Grabbit spanner attachment on his SpyKnife.

'Surf's up!' Zac shouted, squeezing through the hole with his new surfboard tucked under his arm.

He dropped the board onto the steaming water and jumped down on top. He reached up and grabbed the robo-bird, which automatically fastened its claws to the end of the board.

Surfing on boiling water was quite different from ordinary surfing, Zac quickly discovered. There was no room for mistakes.

Better not wipe-out today, he told himself. *Or it'll be hot Zac soup on the menu!*

The river moved quickly, with Zac expertly guiding the board around rocks and bends. The tunnel roof got so low in places that sometimes Zac had to bend right down to avoid hitting his head.

All around him, water heaved and swirled like red-hot porridge. Splashes of scalding hot water sprayed up. Luckily, Zac's cargos were made of heat-resistant cotton.

It was tough surfing, but Zac was practically a pro. He didn't plan to fall off!

Finally, the boiling river gushed out into a huge cavern. A dead end!

Zac glanced up. His head-torch lit up something round and metallic way above him. *A manhole cover!* realised Zac. *If I can get up there, I'll be out! But how exactly do I do that?*

He checked the SpiderPak. Its nanotube silk levels were very low.

Let's hope there's enough to reach up there, thought Zac, pushing the eject button.

ZAP!

The final length of nanotube shot out and stuck to the roof, just as Zac had hoped – right next to the manhole cover.

Zac hauled himself up the line. Then he pushed the cover off and scrambled through, holding the robo-bird.

Zac found himself in a brightly-lit laboratory filled with gadgets, machinery and TV screens.

'I bet Dr Drastic's behind this,' Zac muttered, looking around.

'Actually, Zac,' said a horribly familiar voice, 'Dr Drastic is behind *you*.'

CHAPTER... ...NINE

Zac spun around. Sure enough, he found himself staring into the cold blue eyes of Dr Drastic.

He was as pale as ever, and his hair looked even crazier than the last time Zac had met him. Dr Drastic was clutching the largest remote control Zac had ever seen.

'Thought you'd cured me of evilness, didn't you, Zac?' Dr Drastic chortled.

'Well, I'm so evil that your cure wore off after a month! Now, be a good boy while I tie you to this chair.'

WILD SAVANNAH RESEARCH LAB
ACCESS PASS

DR Drastic

DR VICTOR DRASTIC
PURPLE DIAMOND TECHNOLOGY

Zac let Dr Drastic tie him to an office chair with wheels, and roll him across the laboratory. Sometimes it was good to pretend to be helpless.

Zac saw a clock on the wall beside him. 2.28pm! There was only half an hour left before the deadline!

He knew he'd be able to get out of the ropes – Zac had topped his Escape Artistry class at Spy School, after all. He just didn't know how he was going to stop Dr Drastic's evil plan.

Zac scanned the room. The LaserBlaster had to be around here somewhere. Dr Drastic caught him looking around.

'Allow me to show you my latest creation,' he said, with an icy smile. 'I call it *The Fantastic-Drastic LaserBlaster!*'

Dr Drastic pressed his remote control and a panel in the wall slid open. Hidden behind was the most incredible-looking machine Zac had ever seen.

The barrel of the LaserBlaster was at least two metres wide, and was made of highly polished stainless steel. At the front was a convex lens.

'I got the idea for the design from my own glass eye,' said Dr Drastic, popping his left eye out. 'Brilliant, isn't it? Can you see what I've used for the pupil?'

'Purple diamonds!' gasped Zac, noticing the cluster of glimmering purple gems at the centre of the LaserBlaster's lens.

The LaserBlaster was huge. Zac hated to think how powerful the shockwave would be! *I have to stop him!*

'Purple diamonds indeed,' smirked Dr Drastic. 'I tried to buy the mine, but when the owners refused to sell, I decided to *undermine* them.' Dr Drastic gave a creepy laugh at his lame joke.

'The hardest part was creating the tunnel that led to one of the deserted buildings next to the mine. I had to start it 100 kilometres away so no-one would realise what I was up to. But once that was

done, I was able to set up this laboratory.
I even brought a year's supply of chocolate
bars, so I wouldn't need to leave the lab.
My robo-birds have been hard at work since
we arrived, collecting all the diamonds
I need.'

'Collecting?' snorted Zac. 'You mean
stealing!'

Dr Drastic shrugged. 'Whatever. I only
need one more diamond now. And
I see you've brought
a full robo-bird
with you.'

Dr Drastic
whistled sharply
and the robo-bird

flew over. The bird spat out the purple diamond onto Dr Drastic's hand.

Dr Drastic carefully fitted the diamond into the lens. Instantly, the LaserBlaster began to hum with power.

Dr Drastic's finger started tapping lightly on a big, red button in the centre of his remote control.

I bet that's the activation button, thought Zac nervously. It looked like Dr Drastic was dying to push it!

'What's so great about this thing anyway?' asked Zac, trying to buy some time. He'd almost managed to free one leg from the ropes.

Luckily, Dr Drastic was keen to boast

about his creation.

'My LaserBlaster isn't *great*. It's pure *genius*!' said Dr Drastic, with a mean smile. 'Why, just one shockwave from this beauty will instantly fry every mobile phone around the world. Lines of communication will be so scrambled it'll take *years* to fix them!'

Zac pictured the chaos this would cause. It could bring the world to a standstill!

'But *why?*' he asked.

Dr Drastic scowled. 'I hate those stupid phones. Everyone blah-blah-blahing away on them all the time! Silly text messages! The ridiculous ring-tones! What's wrong with writing letters, like we used to in the olden days? So I'm going to force people to do just that!'

'You're as bad as ever,' Zac growled.

'Thank you!' replied Dr Drastic, with a cackle. 'Actually, I think I'm even *worse* than before. But enough chit-chat,' he said, glancing up at the clock. It was seven minutes to 3pm. 'I have an important deadline to meet.'

CHAPTER... ...TEN

Dr Drastic pressed a button on his remote and the TV screens on the opposite wall flicked on. The worried-looking members of the World Council came into view.

Dr Drastic looked at them coldly. 'So, ladies and gents. Where is my money?' he said, with a frosty politeness.

'We don't pay blackmail,' replied the spokesperson for the Council.

'Fine,' snapped Dr Drastic. 'But if you think your famous boy spy is going to help you out, you're sadly mistaken.'

He rolled Zac forward so the Council could see him. Their faces fell. It seemed like they had just given up all hope of stopping the shockwave.

Zac looked longingly at the remote in Dr Drastic's hand.

'Judging from their faces, I'd say you've just been given the chop!' sneered Dr Drastic to Zac. 'Maybe you could take up a paper-round instead?'

The chop...thought Zac, wriggling his now-untied right foot.

A plan was forming in Zac's head.

Unfortunately, there was no time to decide if it was a good one or not. He just had to hope it worked!

'Aaand…it's 3pm!' announced Dr Drastic, as the clock ticked over. 'Shock-wave time!'

Dr Drastic pointed the remote control at the LaserBlaster.

It was now or never! Zac pushed off the ground with his free leg, spinning across the floor towards Dr Drastic.

Luckily, Dr Drastic was concentrating so hard on his LaserBlaster that he didn't see Zac zooming towards him on the chair.

'Take that!' yelled Zac, karate-chopping Dr Drastic in the back of the knees.

With a cry, Dr Drastic toppled over. The remote control went flying out of his hands and somersaulted through the air.

Zac pushed off and sped along below it, desperately trying to free one of his hands. He had to catch that remote! If it hit the ground, the LaserBlaster might self-activate!

Zac's heart skipped a beat as he realised Dr Drastic was already back on his feet. Finally, with one last twist, Zac wrenched his hand out of the ropes. He reached out and caught the remote. *Yes!*

'Give me that!' yelled Dr Drastic, lunging at Zac.

Swiftly, Zac stuck out his foot. It wasn't

exactly a high-tech approach, but it worked. Dr Drastic tripped over again and skidded along the floor, sliding head-first into the open manhole, his arms pinned to his side! He was stuck fast!

Too many chocolate bars, grinned Zac to himself.

'Hey!' yelled Dr Drastic, kicking his legs in the air. 'Get me out of here!'

'Certainly,' replied Zac. 'But first, let me just shut off this thing forever.'

He examined the remote, and pressed the button labelled 'self-destruct'.

Straight away, the machine began shuddering and making a loud, humming noise. Then the lens at its centre began to twirl around, faster and faster.

The lens exploded and hundreds of tiny purple diamonds sprayed through the air.

SHATTER

The LaserBlaster gave one last wheeze and then went completely silent.

Zac grinned. 'I think it's safe to say that this gadget won't be frying any phones,' he said, as the World Council cheered on the screen behind him.

Zac pulled out his SpyPad and made a quick call.

'Agent Tripwire? Mission complete,' Zac reported. 'Criminal has been identified as Dr Drastic, and LaserBlaster has been deactivated. Please send the GIB arrest crew over here to finish up.'

'Nice work, Agent Rock Star,' said Agent Tripwire.

For once he actually sounded pleased. Maybe Zac was finally getting some of the respect he deserved!

Just then, his SpyPad beeped. *Probably a thank you message from headquarters,* thought Zac. *For, like, single-handedly saving the world. Again!*

But instead, it was a message from his mum.

Zac rolled his eyes. *Maybe I should've let Dr Drastic destroy all the mobile phones, after all!* he grinned to himself.

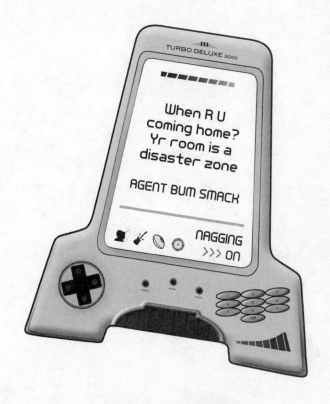

... **THE END** ...

MISSION CHECKLIST
How many have you read?

POISON ISLAND 1

DEEP WATERS 2

MIND GAMES 3

FROZEN FEAR 4

TOMB OF DOOM 5

NIGHT RAID 6

LUNAR STRIKE 7

SUDDEN DROP 8

BLOCKBUSTER 9

SHOCKWAVE 10

HIGH RISK 11

UNDERCOVER 12

SKY HIGH 13

VOLCANIC PANIC 14

BOOT CAMP 15

SWAMP RACE 16

HORROR HOUSE 17

THRILL RIDE 18

CLOSE SHAVE 19

SHIPWRECK 20